Love Among the Lions by F. Anstey

F. Anstey was the pseudonym of Thomas Anstey Guthrie who was born in Kensington, London on August 8th, 1856, to Augusta Amherst Austen, an organist and composer, and Thomas Anstey Guthrie., a prosperous military tailor

Anstey was educated at King's College School and then at Trinity Hall, Cambridge. Although his education was first rate Anstey could only manage a third-class degree; A Gentlemen's degree as it was euphemistically known.

In 1880 he was called to the bar. However this career path rapidly fell away in his desire to become an author. The successful publication of Vice Versa, in 1882, with the premise of a substitution of a father for his schoolboy son, made his name and reputation as a refreshing and original humorist.

The following year he published a rather more serious work, The Giant's Robe. Interestingly the story is about a plagiarist and Anstey was, ironically, accused of plagiarism in writing the work. Despite good reviews both he and his public knew that his writing career was to be that of a humorist.

In the following years he published prolifically beginning with; The Black Poodle (1884), The Tinted Venus (1885), A Fallen Idol (1886), and Baboo Jabberjee B.A. (1897).

Anstey worked not only as a novelist and short story writer but was also a valued member of the staff at the humorous Punch magazine, in which his voces populi and his parodies of a reciter's stock-piece (Burglar Bill) represent perhaps his best work.

In 1901, his successful farce, The Man from Blankleys, based on a story that originally appeared in Punch, was first produced on stage at the Prince of Wales Theatre, in London.

Anstey had become a writer, and a successful one at that, of many talents.

Many more of his stories were made into plays and films over the years. Others were simply taken for the premise alone, usually with no credit to the original author.

By the end of the First World War Anstey's original publications had slowed to a crawl and he seemed rather more interested in translating and publishing some works of Moliere.

Thomas Anstey Guthrie died of pneumonia on March 10th, 1934 in London.

His self-deprecating autobiography, A Long Retrospect, was published in 1936.

Index of Contents

In the following pages will be found the only authentic account of an affair which provided London, and indeed all England, with material for speculation and excitement for a period of at least nine days.

So many inaccurate versions have been circulated, so many ill-natured and unjust aspersions have been freely cast, that it seemed advisable for the sake of those principally concerned to make a plain unvarnished statement of the actual facts. And when I mention that I who write this am the Theodore Blenkinsop whose name was, not long since, as familiar in the public mouth as household words, I venture to think that I shall at once recall the matter to the shortest memory, and establish my right to speak with authority on the subject.

At the time I refer to I was—and for the matter of that still am—employed at a lucrative salary as taster to a well-known firm of tea-merchants in the City. I occupied furnished apartments, a sitting-room and bedroom, over a dairy establishment in Tadmor Terrace, near Baalbec Road, in the pleasant and salubrious district of Highbury.

Arrived at the age of twenty-eight, I was still a bachelor and had felt no serious inclination to change my condition until the memorable afternoon on which the universe became transformed for me in the course of a quiet stroll round Canonbury Square.

For the information of those who may be unacquainted with it, I may state that Canonbury Square is in Islington; the houses, though undeniably dingy as to their exteriors, are highly respectable, and mostly tenanted by members of the medical, musical, or scholastic professions; some have balconies and verandahs which make it difficult to believe that one has not met them, like their occupiers, at some watering place in the summer.

The square is divided into two by a road on which frequent tramcars run to the City, and the two central enclosures are neatly laid out with gravelled paths and garden seats; in the one there is a dovecot, in the other there are large terra-cotta oil-jars, bringing recollections of the Arabian Nights and the devoted Morgiana.

All this, I know, is not strictly to the point, but I am anxious to make it clear that the locality, though not perhaps a chosen haunt of Rank and Fashion, possesses compensations of its own.

Strolling round Canonbury Square, then, I happened to glance at a certain ground floor window in which an art-pot, in the form of a chipped egg hanging in gilded chains and enamelled shrimp-pink, gave a note of femininity that softened the dusty severity of a wire blind.

Under the chipped egg, and above the top of the blind, gazing out with an air of listless disdain and utter weariness, was a lovely vivid face, which, with its hint of pent-up passion and tropical languor, I mentally likened to a pomegranate flower; not that I have ever seen a pomegranate flower, though I am more familiar with the fruit—which, to my palate, has too much the flavour of firewood to be wholly agreeable—but somehow it seemed the only appropriate comparison.

After that, few days passed on which I did not saunter at least once round the square, and several times I was rewarded by the sight of that same exquisite face, looking out over the wire blind, always with the same look of intense boredom and haughty resentment of her surroundings—a kind of modern Mariana, with an area to represent the moat.

I was hopelessly in love from the very first; I thought of nothing but how to obtain admission to her presence; as time went on, I fancied that when I passed there was a gleam of recognition, of half-awakened interest in her long-lashed eyes, but it was difficult to be certain. On the railing by the door was a large brass plate, on which was engraved: "Æneas Polkinghorne, Professor of Elocution. Prospectus within." So I knew the name of my divinity. I can give no greater indication of the extent of my passion, even at this stage, than by saying that I found this surname musical, and lingered over each syllable with delight.

But that brought me no nearer to her, and at last a plan occurred to me by which the abyss of the area that separated us might possibly be bridged over. Nothing could be simpler than my device—and yet there was an audacity about it that rather startled me at first. It was this: the brass plate said "Prospectus within." Very well, all I had to do was to knock boldly and ask for one, which, after some natural hesitation, I did.

Any wild hope of obtaining an interview with Miss Polkinghorne was doomed to instant disappointment. I was received by the Professor himself, a tall, stout, flabby person, with sandy hair combed back over his brow and worn long behind, who showed a most sympathetic interest in me, inquiring whether I wished to be prepared for the Church, the Stage, or the Bar, or whether I had any idea of entering Parliament. I fear I allowed him to suppose the latter, although I am about as likely to get into Parliament as into an imperial pint measure; but I had to say something to account for my visit, and the tea-trade does not call for much in the way of oratorical skill from its votaries.

Our interview was brief, but I came away, not only with a prospectus, but with tickets, for which I paid cash, entitling me to a course of six lessons in elocution.

This was rather more than I had calculated upon—but, at least, it gave me the entrée to the house, and it might lead to something more.

It did not seem as if it was going to lead to much; the Professor's method of teaching was peculiar: he would post me in a study at the back of the house, where I was instructed to declaim some celebrated oration at the top of my voice while he retired upstairs to discover how far my voice would carry.

After twenty minutes or so he would return with the information, which I have no reason to disbelieve, that he had not heard a single word above the first landing.

Still I persevered, sustained by the thought that, when I was delivering the oration of Brutus over Cæsar, or the famous passage about the Queen of France and the "ten thousand swords leaping from their scabbards," my words might perchance reach Miss Polkinghorne's ear and excite in her a passing emotion.

But I came to the end of my tickets and still I was as far as ever from my goal, while the exertion of shouting had rendered me painfully husky.

Yet I would not give in; I set myself to gain the Professor's good opinion; I took more tickets. It was not till after I had run through these that I ascertained, by an apparently careless inquiry, that there was no such person as Miss Polkinghorne—the Professor was a widower and had never had a daughter!

The thought that I had wasted so much time and money for nothing was bitter at first, and I very nearly decided to discontinue my studies there and then. But I conquered my feelings. Though the Professor was no relation to this young lady, he must know her name, he must be able to give me some information about her; a little judicious pumping might render him communicative.

"My dear Sir," he said, after I had been beating about the bush for some time with cautious delicacy, "I think I understand. You are anxious to make this young lady's acquaintance with a view to paying your addresses to her? Is not that so?"

I confessed that he had managed to penetrate my motives, though I could not imagine how.

"You will not be the first who has sought to win Lurana's affections," he said; "more than one of my pupils—but the child is ambitious, difficult to please. Unfortunately, this is your final lesson—otherwise I might, after preparing the ground, so to say, have presented you to her, and I daresay she would have been pleased to give you a cup of tea occasionally after your labours. Indeed, as Miss Lurana de Castro's stepfather, I can answer for that—however, since our acquaintance unhappily ceases here——"

It did not cease there; I took another dozen tickets at once, and if even Polkinghorne had sounded sweetly to my enamoured ear, you may conceive what enchanting melody lay in a name so romantic and so euphonious as Lurana de Castro.

The Professor was as good as his word; at the end of the very next lesson I was invited to follow him to the drawing-room, where I found the owner of the brilliant face that had so possessed me seated at her tea-table.

She gave me a cup of tea, and I can pay her witchery no higher compliment when I state that it seemed to me as nectar, even though my trained palate detected in it an inartistic and incongruous blend of broken teas, utterly without either style or quality. I am not sure that I did not ask for another.

She was astonishingly lovely; her Spanish descent was apparent in her magnificent black tresses, lustrous eyes, and oval face of olive tinted with richest carmine. As I afterwards learnt, she was the daughter of a Spanish Government official of an ancient Castilian family, who had left his widow in such straitened circumstances that she was compelled to support herself by exhibiting performing mice and canaries at juvenile parties, until she met and married the Professor, who at that time was delivering recitations illustrated by an oxy-hydrogen lantern.

The second marriage had not been altogether a success, and, now that the Professor was a widower, I fancy that his relations with his imperious stepdaughter were not invariably of the most cordial nature, and that he would have been grateful to any one who succeeded in winning her hand and freeing him from her sway.

I did not know that then, however, though I was struck by the deferential politeness of his manner towards her, and the alacrity with which, after he had refreshed himself, he shuffled out of the room, leaving Lurana to entertain me single-handed.

That first evening with her was not unmixed joy. I had the consciousness of being on trial. I knew that many had been tried and found wanting before me. Lurana's attitude was languid, indifferent, almost disdainful, and when I went away I had a forlorn conviction that I should never again be asked to tea with her, and that the last series of tickets represented money absolutely thrown away!

And yet I was asked again—not only once, but many times, which was favourable as far as it went, for I felt tolerably certain that the Professor would never have ventured to bring me a second time into his daughter's presence, unless he had been distinctly given to understand that my society was very far from distasteful to her.

As I grew to know her better, I learnt the secret of her listlessness and discontent with life. She was tormented by the unbounded ambitions and the distinct limitations which embitter existence for so many young girls of our day.

The admiration which her beauty excited gave her little satisfaction; such social success as Highbury or Canonbury could offer left her cold and unmoved. She was pining for some distinction which should travel beyond her own narrow little world, and there did not seem to be any obvious way of attaining it. She would not have minded being a popular author or artist—only she could find nothing worth writing about, and she did not know how to draw; she would have loved to be a great actress—but unfortunately she had never been able to commit the shortest part to memory, and the pride of a de Castro forbade her to accept anything but leading rôles.

No wonder that she was devoured by dulness, or that there were moments when she beat her pinions like some captive wild bird against the cage of her own incompetence. Even I, although fairly content with my lot, would sometimes flap my own wings, so to speak, from sheer sympathy.

"It's maddening to be a nobody!" she would declare, as she threw herself petulantly back in her chair, with her arms raised behind her and her interlaced fingers forming a charming cradle for her head—a favourite attitude of hers. "It does seem so stupid not to be celebrated when almost everybody is! And to think that I have a friend like Ruth Rakestraw, who knows ever so many editors and people, and could make me famous with a few strokes of the pen—if only I did something to give her the chance. But I never do!"

Miss Rakestraw, I should explain, was an enterprising young lady journalist, who contributed society news and "on dits" to the leading Islington and Holloway journals, and was understood to have had "leaderettes" and "turnovers" accepted by periodicals of even greater importance.

"If only," Lurana burst out on one of these occasions, "if only I could do something once which would get my name into all the papers, set everybody thinking of me, talking of me, staring after me wherever I went, make editors write for my photograph, and interviewers beg for my biography, I think I should be content."

I made the remark, which was true but not perhaps startling in its originality, that fame of this kind was apt to be of brief duration.

"What should I care?" she cried; "I should have had it. I could keep the cuttings; they would always be there to remind me that once at least—but what's the use of talking? I shall never see my name in all the papers. I know I shan't!"

"There is a way!" I ventured to observe; "you might have your name in all the papers, if you married."

"As if I meant that!" she said, with a deliciously contemptuous pout. "And whom should I marry, if you please, Mr Blenkinsop?"

"You might marry me!" I suggested humbly.

"You!" she retorted. "How would that make me a celebrity. You are not even one yourself."

"I do not care to boast," I said, "but it is the simple fact that nobody in the entire tea-trade has a palate approaching mine for keenness and delicacy. Ask any one and they will tell you the same."

"You may be the best tea-taster in the world," she said, "but the purity of your palate will never gain you a paragraph in a single society paper. And even if it did, what should I gain? At the best a reflected glory. I want to be a somebody myself!"

"What's the use of trying to make ourselves what we are not?" I broke out. "If Fate has made us wooden ninepins in the world's nursery, we may batter our head against the walls as much as we like—but we can never batter it into a profile!"

I thought this rather neatly put myself, but it did not appeal to Miss de Castro, who retorted with some asperity that I was the best judge of the material of my own head, but hers, at least, was not wooden, while she had hitherto been under the impression that it already possessed a profile—such as it was.

She could not be brought to understand that I was merely employing a metaphor, and for the remainder of the evening her demeanour was so crushingly chilling, that I left in the lowest spirits, persuaded that my unlucky tongue had estranged me from Lurana for ever.

For some time I avoided Canonbury Square altogether, for I felt unequal to facing an elocution lesson unrecompensed by tea with Miss de Castro, and the halfhour or more of delightful solitude à deux which followed the meal—for it had never occurred to the Professor to provide his stepdaughter with a chaperon.

At last, when on the verge of despair, hope returned in the form of a little note from Lurana, asking whether I was dead, and inviting me, if still in existence, to join a small party to visit the World's Fair at the Agricultural Hall the next evening, and return to supper afterwards at Canonbury Square, an invitation which, need I say, I joyfully accepted.

We were only four; Miss Rakestraw and her fiancé, a smart young solicitor's clerk, of the name of Archibald Chuck, whose employer had lately presented him with his articles; myself, and Lurana. The Professor was unable to accompany us, having an engagement to read "Hiawatha" to a Young Men's Mutual Improvement Society that evening.

Part of the hall was taken up by various side-shows, shooting-galleries, and steam merry-go-rounds, which produced a discordant and deafening din until a certain hour of the evening, when the noises subsided, and Wooker and Sawkins' World-renowned Circus gave a performance in the arena, which occupied the centre.

Miss Rakestraw's connection with the Press procured us free passes to the reserved seats close to the ring; my chair was next to Lurana's, and she was graciously pleased to ignore our recent difference. The entertainment was of the usual variety, I suppose; but, to tell the truth, I was so absorbed in the bliss of being once more by her side and watching her face, which looked more dazzling than ever through the delicate meshes of her veil, that I have the vaguest recollection of the earlier items of the programme.

But towards the close there came a performance which I have good reason to remember.

An enormous elephant entered the circle, drawing a trolley, upon which was an iron cage containing forest-bred African lions. After the electric globes had been lowered, so as to illuminate the interior, "Niono, the Lion King," a dapper, wellmade man, of very much my own height and figure, so far as I could judge, went into the cage and put the animals through various exercises. Niono was succeeded by Mlle. Léonie, the "Circe of the Carnivora," a pretty Frenchwoman, who, as it seemed to me, surpassed him in coolness and daring. There was nothing disagreeably sensational about the exhibition; all the animals were evidently under perfect control; the huge, black-maned lions leaped through paper hoops and blazing circles without the slightest loss of either temper or dignity; the females followed obediently. Only one lioness showed any disposition to be offensive, and she did not venture to go beyond yawning ostentatiously whenever Mlle. Léonie's eye was upon her.

Altogether it was, as I remarked to Lurana at the time, a wonderful instance of the natural dominion of man over the animal world. She enthusiastically commended the symmetry of Mr Niono's figure, which did not strike me as so very much above the average; and to pique her, I expressed equal admiration for Mlle. Léonie, and was gratified to observe unmistakable signs of jealousy on Lurana's part. But we were both agreed that the profession of lion-taming looked more dangerous than it actually was, and Archibald Chuck mentioned that some townsman in the provinces had, for a very trifling wager, entered a den of lions in a travelling menagerie with perfect impunity. Miss Rakestraw capped this by a case from America, in which a young couple had actually chosen a lion's cage to be married in, though she admitted that the story was possibly a fabrication.

I walked back with Lurana alone, as we somehow lost sight of Mr Chuck and his fiancée in the crush going out, and on the way home I could not refrain from pleading my cause once more. I told her how I had loved her at first sight, and how many elocution lessons I had endured for her sake; I pointed out that I was already receiving a salary sufficient to maintain a wife in comfort, if not luxury; and that her married life could hardly be more monotonous and uncongenial than her present existence.

She listened attentively, as if moved. Presently she said, "Theodore, I will be perfectly frank. I do like you; I believe I could even love you. But I have Spanish blood in my veins. I could never be satisfied with a humdrum conventional marriage."

I was inexpressibly shocked. I had no idea that her views were so emancipated.

"Lurana," I said, "believe me, never mind what the lady novelists say against marriage; it may have its disadvantages, but, after all, as society is constituted—"

"You don't understand," she said. "I am not opposed to marriage—with a man who is willing to make some concession, some slight sacrifice, to gratify me. But are you that kind of man, Theodore, I wonder?"

I saw that she was already beginning to yield. "I would do anything—anything in the world you bid me," I cried, "if only you will be my wife, Lurana."

"I should ask you to do nothing that I am not perfectly prepared to do myself," she said. "A temporary inconvenience, a risk which is the merest trifle. Still, you may think it too much, Theodore."

"Name it," I replied. "The opportunities which the tea trade affords for the cultivation of heroism are rare; but there are few risks that I would shrink from running with you."

"It is only this," she said. "I don't want a commonplace wedding. I want one that will be talked about and make a sensation. Will you let me be married in my own way?"

I was rather relieved by what seemed so moderate a demand. "Certainly, darling," I said; "we will be married in Westminster Abbey, by the Archbishop of Canterbury, if you wish it, and it can be arranged. What matter where or how the ceremony take place, or what it costs, provided it makes you mine for ever?"

"Then, Theodore," she said, pressing my arm impulsively with her slim fingers, while the rays of a street lamp in the square fell on her upturned face and shining eyes, "let us be married at the Agricultural Hall—in the Lions' Cage!"

I confess to being considerably startled. I had expected something rather out of the common, but nothing in the least like this.

"In the lions' cage!" I repeated, blankly. "Wouldn't that be rather smelly, Lurana? And, besides, the menagerie people would never lend it for such a purpose. Where would they put the lions, you know?"

"Why, the lions would be there, of course," she said, "or else there'd be nothing in it."

"If I am to be married in a lion-cage," I said, with a very feeble attempt at levity, "I should very much prefer that there was nothing in it."

"Ah, you may laugh, Theodore!" she said, "but, after all your professions, surely you won't refuse the very first indulgence I ask! You may think it a mere whim, a girlish caprice; but understand this—I am thoroughly in earnest about it. If you are willing to marry me as I wish, the wedding may be as soon as ever you please. But if not, tell me so plainly, and let us part for ever. Either I will be married in my own way, or not at all."

What could I do? It was simply impossible to give her up now, the very moment after she was won. And to lose her for such a mere punctilio; for, of course, this condition of hers was too fantastic to be practicable; the Professor would certainly refuse his consent to so eccentric a ceremony; Lurana herself would probably realise before long the absurdity of the idea. In the meantime, as her acknowledged fiancé, I should have the immense advantage of being on the spot when she returned to a more reasonable frame of mind.

So I gave way, and assured her that I had no personal objection to lions, and would as soon be married in their presence as elsewhere, provided that we could obtain the necessary permission; and even if I had thought this more probable than I did, I believe—so potent was the witchery of Lurana's voice and eyes—I should have said precisely the same.

"Dearest Theodore!" she murmured, "I never really doubted you. I felt so sure that you would be nice and sympathetic about it. If we couldn't agree about such a trifling thing as where we are to be married, we should be unsuited to one another, shouldn't we? Now we will just walk round the square once more, and then go in and tell the others what we have arranged."

They had sat down to supper when we entered, and the Professor cast a glance of keen inquiry through his spectacles at us, over the cold beef and pickles with which he was recruiting his energies after "Hiawatha."

"Yes, papa," said Lurana, calmly, "we are a little late; but Theodore has been asking me to marry him, and I have said I would."

There was an outburst of congratulations from Miss Rakestraw and Chuck. Old Polkinghorne thought fit to conceal his joy under a cloak of stagey emotion. "Well, well," he said, "it is Nature's law; the young birds spread their wings and quit the warm nest, and the old ones are left to sit and brood over the past. I cannot blame you, child. As for you, my boy," he added, extending a flabby hand to me, "all I can say is, there is no one to whom I would so willingly surrender her."

There was scarcely any one to whom, in my opinion, he would not surrender her with the utmost alacrity, for, as I have already hinted, Lurana, with all her irresistible fascination, had a temper of her own, and was apt to make the parental nest a trifle too warm for the elder bird occasionally.

"And when am I to lose my sunbeam?" he asked. "Not just yet?"

"Theodore wishes to have the marriage as soon as possible," said Lurana, "by special licence."

"Have you settled where?" inquired Miss Rakestraw, with feminine interest in such details.

"Well," said Lurana slowly, evidently enjoying the effect she was producing, "Theodore and I have quite made up our minds to be married at the Menagerie—in the den of lions."

"How splendid!" exclaimed the lady journalist. "It's never been done over here. What a sensation it will make! I'll do a full descriptive report for all my papers!"

"That's what I call a real sporting way of getting spliced," said Chuck. "Only wish I'd thought of it myself before I had our banns put up, Ruth. First-rate idea of yours, Blenkinsop."

"Of course," I said, "if the Professor thinks it in the least unsafe—"

"Oh, it's safe enough," put in Chuck, who was a little too apt to volunteer his opinion. "Why, we've seen the lions, Professor; they're as quiet as lambs. And anyway, they'd have the lion-tamer in with them, you know. They'll be all right!"

"I think," said the Professor, "we may disregard the danger; but the expense—have you thought what it will cost, Theodore?"

"I have not," I said, "not till you mentioned it. It will probably be enormous, more than I could possibly afford—unless you are ready to go halves?" I concluded, feeling perfectly certain that he was ready to do nothing of the sort.

"But look here," said Chuck, "why should it cost you anything? If you go the right way about it, you ought to get all your expenses paid by the circus, and a share of the gate-money into the bargain."

"Oh, Mr Chuck!" cried Lurana, "how clever of you to think of that! wasn't it, Theodore?"

I could have kicked Chuck, but I said it was a stroke of positive genius.

"That's simple enough," he said. "The rock I see ahead is getting the special licence. You see, if you want to marry anywhere else than in a certified place of worship or a registry office, you must first satisfy the Archbishop of Canterbury, or the Surrogate, or whoever the old Josser is at Doctors' Commons who looks after these things, that it's a 'convenient place' within the Marriage Act of 1836. Now, the point is, will a cage of lions strike them as coming under that description?"

If it should, the ecclesiastical notions of convenience must be more than peculiar. For the first time I realised what an able fellow Chuck was.

"My dear Chuck!" I said, "what a marvellous knowledge you have of law! You've hit the weak spot. It would be perfectly hopeless to make such an application. It's a pity, but we must give it up, that's all— we must give it up."

"Then," said Lurana, "we must give up any marriage at all, for I certainly don't intend to marry anywhere else."

"After all," said the irrepressible Chuck, "all you need apply for is a licence to marry in the Agricultural Hall; they won't want to know the exact spot. I tell you what, you go and talk it over with the circus people and fix the day, and I'll go up to Doctors' Commons and get round 'em somehow. You leave it to me."

"Do you know," said the Professor, beaming, "I really begin to think this idea of yours can be carried out quite comfortably after all, Theodore. It certainly has the attraction of novelty, besides being safe, and even, it may be, remunerative. To a true lover, a lions' cage may be as fit a temple of Hymen as any other structure, and their roars be gentle as the ring-dove's coo. Go and see these people the first thing tomorrow, and no doubt you will be able to come to terms with them."

This I agreed to do, and Lurana insisted on coming with me. Miss Rakestraw was in ecstasies over our proposal, and undertook to what she called "boom the wedding for all it was worth" in every paper with which she had any connection, and with other more influential organs to which the possession of such exclusive intelligence as hers would procure her the entrée.

By the end of the evening she had completely turned Lurana's head, and even I myself was not quite untouched by the general enthusiasm. It seemed to me that being married in a den of lions might not be such bad fun after all.

When I awoke next morning with the dawning recollection of what I was in for, the glamour had in a great measure departed from the idea, which seemed to me at best but a foolish piece of bravado. It had been arranged that I should call for Lurana immediately after breakfast, and interview the circus proprietors on my way to business, and I rather expected to find that the night had borne counsel to her as well as myself; but she was in exuberant spirits, and as keen about the project as ever, so I thought it better not to betray that my own ardour had abated.

But what, after all, were we going to request? That these people should allow their lions to be inconvenienced, quite unnecessarily, by a wedding in their cage between two perfect strangers who had all London to choose from!

I believed that they would decline to entertain the suggestion for a moment, and, if so, I could not blame them. I felt that they would have both right and reason on their side.

On arriving at the Hall, we inquired for Mr Wooker or Mr Sawkins, and were requested to wait, which we did in a draughty passage smelling strongly of stables, while loud snorting and wheezing reached our ears from the arena, where they seemed to be exercising the circus stud.

At last we were told that Mr Sawkins would see us (I don't know to this day whether Mr Wooker had any real existence or not), and were shown up to his office, which did not differ from any other office, except that it had a gaudy circus poster and a bill announcing the sale by auction of some rival menagerie pinned against the wall. As for Mr Sawkins, he was a florid, jowly man, with the remnants of his hair dyed and parted down the middle, a kind of amalgam of a country job-master and the dignified person who bows customers into chairs in a fashionable draper's establishment.

He heard Lurana, who acted as spokeswoman, with magisterial gravity, and, to my surprise, without appearing to regard us as a pair of morbid maniacs.

"There's no denying," he said, "that the thing would draw if properly billed, always supposing, mind you, that it's capable of being done at all. And the only person able to give an opinion about that is Mr Onion, the gentleman," he explained, "who is our Lion King. He spells his name 'Niono' professionally, which gives it more of an African flavour, if you follow my meaning. I'll call down the tube for him."

I awaited Mr Onion's arrival with impatience. He presently made his appearance in a short-braided tunic, with black lamb's wool round the collar and cuffs. By daylight his countenance, though far from ill-looking, was sallow and seamed; there was a glance of admiration in his bold, dark eyes as they rested on Lurana's spirited face.

"Well," he decided, after the case had been explained to him, "if the lady's as game as she seems, and the gentleman likewise, I don't see any objection. Along with me, there'll be no more danger than if it was a cage of white mice—provided you've the nerve for it."

Lurana said proudly that her own mother had been an accomplished animal trainer—she did not mention the kind of animals—and that she herself was quite incapable of being afraid of a lion.

"If you've got nerve," said Mr Niono, "you're right enough, but you can't create it; it's a gift. Take me. I'm hardly ever away from my animals. I get downright impatient for every performance. But if ever I got the feeling that I was afraid of them lions or they weren't afraid o' me, do you think I'd trust myself inside that cage? No fear! They've left their marks on me as it is—my 'trade marks,' as I call 'em—see!" and here he bared his arm and exhibited some fearful scars; "but that's affection, that is."

He then offered to introduce us to his pets, and I should have accompanied Lurana to see the cage, only on the way we met Mlle. Léonie, to whom Mr Sawkins presented me, and, naturally, I was compelled to stop. She was a piquant-looking woman, not quite in her first youth, perhaps, but still attractive, and with the indescribable, airy grace of a Parisian, though I believe she came from Belgium. Mademoiselle was charmed with our project, complimented me upon my Britannic phlegm, and predicted that I should find the little experience "all," as she put it, "that there was of the most agreeable," which I devoutly hoped would be the case.

We were still chatting when Lurana returned, enraptured with the lions, one of whom had actually allowed her to tickle him behind the ear. Niono testified that her nerve, at all events, was beyond question. She was anxious that I should go and tickle the lion, too; but this I declined, being occupied in talking to Mlle. Léonie at the time.

"There's one thing," said Mr Sawkins later, as we were discussing the arrangements, "we shouldn't object to paying for the special licence; but where are you going to find a parson to marry you? You must have a parson of some sort, you know."

Again Fate seemed to have interposed an insurmountable barrier between us and our desire. I had to admit that it would be difficult, if not impossible, to find a clergyman courageous enough to enter the cage with us.

"Well, there's no call for him to be inside of it," said Mr Niono, who was with us, heart and soul, by this time. "In fact, the lady and yourself are about as many as I could undertake to be answerable for. We could rig him up a perch outside to read the service from, comfortable."

Even so, I said, I was afraid that it was hardly a service one could ask any divine to perform.

"I know a party who'd jump at it," said Mr Niono, who was full of resource. "The Reverend Skipworth. You know who I mean, Sawkins. Little chap in a check suit and goggles I introduced to you at the bar the other evening—always dropping in, he is. He'd do it, just for the lark of the thing. And he's a regular professional, you know," he added for my benefit, "though he don't sport a white choker in his off hours; likes to go about and see life for himself, and quite right. You get the licence, sir, and I'll guarantee that the Reverend Ninian Skipworth will do the job for you."

So we left the hall, delighted, especially Lurana, with the unexpected ease with which our object had been attained. It had seemed at first the wildest extravagance, and now there was apparently every prospect that Lurana and I would really exchange our marriage vows in a den of forest-bred lions, unless (which, of course, was a possibility that had to be taken into account) the ecclesiastical authorities should refuse to grant a special licence.

I was unable to apply in person at Doctors' Commons, for Lurana insisted that I should leave the whole matter in Chuck's hands, but I impressed upon him the necessity of absolute candour with the officials.

Whether he told them all, whether they were remiss in making full inquiry, or whether—as I would rather not think—he intentionally deceived them, I cannot say, but at all events he came back triumphantly with the special licence.

Wooker and Sawkins had fixed an early date, and wished the wedding to take place at night, so as to figure in the evening programme, but the Surrogate, or somebody at the office, had insisted that it must be in the afternoon, which would, of course, oblige Mr Sawkins to introduce it at a matinée performance.

Miss Rakestraw proved herself a born journalist. She placed her news at the disposal of an enterprising evening journal, whose bills that very same evening came out with startling and alliterative headlines such as:

LOVE LAUGHS AT LIONS!

Canonbury Couple to Marry in Cageful of Carnivora.

and from that moment, as the reader will recollect, Lurana and I became public characters.

There were portraits—quite unrecognisable—of us in several of the illustrated weeklies, together with sketches of and interviews with us both, contributed by Miss Ruth's facile stylograph, and an account of the Professor, contributed by himself.

As for the daily papers there was scarcely one, from the Times downwards, which did not contain a leader, a paragraph, or a letter on the subject of our contemplated wedding. Some denounced me violently for foolhardy rashness, others for the selfishness with which I was encouraging an impressionable girl to risk her life to gratify my masculine vanity. Several indignantly demanded whether it was true that the Archbishop had sanctioned such a scandalous abuse of marriage rites, and if so, what the Home Office were about?

There was a risk that all this publicity would end in the authorities being compelled to interfere and countermand the ceremony, and yet I cannot honestly say that I disliked the fuss that was made about it. In the City, to be sure, I had to put up with a certain amount of chaff; facetious inquiries as to whether I intended to present the leonine bridesmaids with bones or pieces of raw meat, and the precise locality in which my wife and I thought of spending our honeymoon. But such badinage covered a very genuine respect for my intrepidity, and I was looked upon as a credit to the tea trade.

The appointed day was getting nearer and nearer, and still—so wonderfully did Fortune befriend us— the authorities gave no sign of any intention to interfere. Parliament had not yet reassembled, so no one could rise and put a question in the House to the Home Secretary, and if Government officials ever read the morning papers, it seemed that they did not feel called upon to take cognisance of anything they read there, unless compelled to do so by pressure from without.

Nor did the Archbishop take any steps. No doubt he may have been unaware of the precise conditions under which the ceremony was to be sanctioned, and the same remark applies to the Bishop of London. It is true that their attention was drawn to the facts by more than one postcard, as I have reason to know. But some people make a practice—and it is not for me to condemn them—of taking no notice of anonymous communications.

However, as the time drew on, I thought it would be only proper on my part to go and call upon the Reverend Ninian Skipworth, the curate with whom our energetic friend, Mr Niono, had now made all the necessary arrangements, and find out, quietly, what his state of mind was. He might be wavering, in which case I should have to strengthen his resolution. Or he might not yet have realised all the possible consequences of his good nature, and if so, I should not be acting fairly towards him if I did not lay them before him, even though the result should be that he withdrew from his engagement.

Niono had given me his address, and I looked in at the curate's unpretentious lodgings one evening on my way home. I found him in, and as soon as he learnt my name, he offered me whisky and soda and a cigar with most unparsonical joviality.

The Reverend Ninian, I found, was a cleric of the broad-minded school which scorns conventional restrictions; he held that if the Church was to maintain its influence, it must follow the trend of modern progress, and neglect no opportunity of winning the hearts of the people. He was only sorry, he told me, that the prejudices of his Bishop would prevent him from reading the service inside the cage.

I replied gratefully that I was sufficiently indebted to him as it was, since if his connection with the affair reached the episcopal ear, he would be in serious danger of being suspended, even if he did not receive some still heavier punishment.

"Oh, don't you bother about that!" he said, cheerily; "it's awfully good of you to trouble yourself on my account; but if the Bishop is such an old stick-in-the-mud as to haul me up for a little thing like this, I shall simply chuck up the Church altogether, that's all! In fact, I've almost decided to do it in any case, for I believe I could do more real good outside the Establishment than in. And I admire your pluck, my dear fellow, and your manly straightforwardness in coming here like this; and I'm hanged if I don't marry you and chance the consequences, so don't say another word about it."

I didn't, though I need not say I was profoundly moved by the genuine sympathy and assistance which our project seemed to inspire in the most unexpected quarters.

My one anxiety now was about Lurana. Outwardly she appeared cheerful and even gay, and thoroughly to enjoy her position as the heroine of the hour; but how could I be sure that this was genuine and not a highstrung hysterical self-repression which would be succeeded by a violent reaction, it might be in the lions' cage itself?

From that at all hazards she must be saved. Earnestly, seriously, I pointed out how much would depend on her maintaining perfect coolness and composure during the ceremony, and implored her, if she felt the slightest misgivings, the smallest tendency to shrink in secret from the coming ordeal, not to allow any false pride to close her lips. There was still time, I reminded her. If on second thoughts, she preferred to be married in the old time-honoured way, instead of in a Menagerie den, she had only to say so. Her happiness and comfort were the chief things to consider.

"Withdraw now, Theodore?" she said, "after announcing it in all the papers! Why, how could we?"

"I would take all that upon myself," I told her; "I need only say that you don't feel quite equal to facing lions."

"But I do, Theodore," she said, "the dear, ducky, pussy-faced old things! Who could possibly be afraid of lions—especially with Mr Niono to protect us?"

"If you knew more about lions, Lurana," I said, "you would know how liable they are to sudden rages, and how little even lion-tamers themselves—"

"If you go on like that, Theodore," she said, "I shall begin to think that you want to frighten me—and even that you are just a little frightened yourself. But I'm not to be frightened. I should not be my mother's daughter if I had any fear of animals. And once for all, you will either marry me in the lions' cage or not at all!"

I saw that I should only be exposing myself to further misunderstanding if I pursued the subject. Lurana had that quality of courage which springs from a total lack of imagination; she had never seen a performing lion ramp and roar, and it was inconceivable to her that one could ever indulge in such exercises. Still less did she understand that there is another type of courage, which sees all the difficulties and dangers beforehand, even exaggerated by distance, and yet advances calmly and undauntedly to encounter them. My courage was of that sort, and it is generally admitted that it belongs to a far higher order than the other.

Now that the die was cast I found myself anticipating the eventful day with philosophic equanimity. It was an uncomfortable method of getting married, no doubt, but after all, what man ever was comfortable at his own wedding?

And surely one crowded quarter-of-an-hour (for it would certainly be crowded in that cage) of glorious life would be worth an age without Lurana—who was not to be won by any other means.

PART II

It was now the eve of my wedding-day, and it was generally taken for granted that Lurana and I would be allowed to enter the lion-cage without opposition from any quarter.

Whether we should find it as easy to come out again was a point on which opinions differed considerably, but the majority must have been confident that the ceremony would pass off without any unpleasant interruption—for the rush to obtain seats was tremendous.

I was just as tranquil and collected as ever; I could not detect that my valour had "ullaged," as wine-merchants say, in the slightest degree, though Lurana was perpetually questioning me as to whether I was sure I would not rather withdraw.

Of course, I indignantly repudiated the very idea, but it is well known that a perfectly sober person, if suddenly taxed with being drunk, will seem and even feel so, and it is much the same with any imputation of cowardice.

I began to think that constant tea tasting, even though the infusions are not actually swallowed, probably has some subtle effect upon the nervous system, and that it would brace me up and also show me how little cause I had to be uneasy, if I dropped into the Agricultural Hall once more and saw Niono put his lions through their performances.

So I left the City early that afternoon and paid for my admission to the hall like an ordinary sightseer; I did not ask Lurana to accompany me, because I knew she must have plenty to keep her at home just then.

I was just in time for the performing lions, and found a place in the outer edge of the crowd; it was strange to stand there unrecognised and hear myself being freely discussed by all around; strange and decidedly exhilarating, too, to think that in another twenty-four hours I should be, not a spectator of what was to take place in that arena, but one of the principal performers, the centre of breathless interest, the hero of the hour!

But with the appearance of the cage, this unnatural exhilaration suddenly died down. It was not so much the lions, though they struck me as larger and less easy-tempered than on the first occasion, while the lioness was as nearly in open revolt as she dared. What troubled me most was that the cage contained another inmate, one whom I did not remember to have seen before—a magnificent specimen of the Bengal tiger.

It seemed perfectly clear to me that the brute was only about half-trained; he went through his tricks in a sullen perfunctory way, with a savage, snurring snap every now and then, which, even at that distance, made my flesh creep.

And, whenever he snapped, clouds of steam issued from his great jaws; I could see, too, that the lioness was secretly egging him on to fresh acts of defiance, and that he was only watching his opportunity to crouch and spring as soon as Niono's back was turned.

I was perfectly determined that I would not have that tiger at my wedding; he would never keep still for a moment; he would upset all the other animals, and how could I be expected to remain cool with a great, hot, steaming beast like that at my elbow? Why, he must raise the temperature of that cage to the atmosphere of a Turkish bath! For Lurana's sake as well as my own, I really must draw the line at tigers—they were not in the bond.

Another thing that annoyed me was the senseless tomfoolery of the clowns, who persisted in running after the cage at the conclusion of the performance, and teasing the poor defenceless animals by making grimaces and dashing their ridiculous conical hats against the bars. It was painful to think that any one could be found to smile at such cheap buffoonery—if I had been the ring-master, I would have given those cowardly idiots a taste of the whip!

I decided to go round afterwards and see Onion about that tiger.

I did not see the lion-tamer, as he had just left the hall, and Mr Sawkins, I was told, was engaged, but I saw Mlle. Léonie, who was most friendly.

I remarked, carelessly, that I saw they had put a tiger into the cage.

Mademoiselle said he was a member of the troupe, but had been indisposed and temporarily transferred to the hospital cage.

I hinted that a tiger, however convalescent, was hardly a desirable addition to our wedding party. Mademoiselle was astounded; a so gracious beast, a veritable treasure, with him present, the ceremony would have a style, a cachet, an elegance. Without him—ah! bah! it would be triste—banal, tame!

I admitted this, but urged that we were quiet people who wanted to be married as quietly as possible, and that a tiger, for persons in our condition of life, was a ridiculous piece of ostentation. It was always better to begin as one meant to go on.

She differed from me totally. I was too modest, for, of course, it was incredible that I, who was so full of sangfroid, could object to the tiger for any other reason?

"Personally," I replied, "I had no prejudice against tigers whatever—but Mademoiselle would understand that I was bound to consider another person's convenience."

"Not possible!" exclaimed Mademoiselle, "a young lady with so much verve to be timid! Why, Mons. Onion raved of her fearlessness!"

I said it was not timidity in Lurana's case—she merely happened to have an antipathy for tigers. Some people, as Mademoiselle was doubtless aware, were unable to remain in the same room with a cat; Miss de Castro could not stay in the same cage with a tiger—it was temperament.

"Ah," said Mdlle. Hortense, "I understand that. A sensitive?"

"Yes," I said, "a sensitive."

"But Niono says she is one of us!" objected Mademoiselle, "that she was brought up amongst animals—that her mamma was herself an animal-tamer."

"Of white mice and canary birds," I said, "but that is not quite the same thing as tigers, and I am perfectly certain that if that tiger is retained, the wedding will not take place."

Her keen grey eyes flashed with comprehension. Ah, the poor little one! in that case it was another thing. She would speak to the "Patron" and to Mons. Onion; the tiger should not be permitted to trouble the fête. I could rely absolutely upon her—he should be accommodated elsewhere.

I went back to Lurana in a somewhat relieved frame of mind, and when she asked me where I had been, I mentioned, perhaps unwisely, that I had dropped in at the Circus and had a little chat with Mlle. Léonie. I did not say anything about the tiger, because there seemed to be no object in disturbing her, now that the matter was comfortably settled, not to mention that if Lurana had known I had directed the removal of the tiger without consulting her, she was quite self-willed enough to insist on his immediate restoration to the lion-cage.

Most girls would have been impressed by my courage in going near the Circus at all at such a time; not so Lurana, who pretended to believe that Mlle. Léonie was the attraction.

"Oh, I noticed she was making eyes at you from the very beginning," she declared; "you had better marry her, and then Mr Niono could marry me. I daresay he would have no objection."

"My darling," I said, gently, "do not let us quarrel the very last evening we may spend together on earth."

"You might take a more cheerful view of it than that, Theodore!" she exclaimed.

"I think you are a little inclined to treat it too lightly," I replied. "I have been studying those lions, Lurana, and it is my deliberate opinion that they are in a condition of suppressed excitement which will break out on the slightest pretext. Unless you can trust yourself to meet their gaze without faltering, without so much as a flicker of the eyelid you will, unless I am greatly mistaken, stand a considerable chance of being torn to pieces."

"Nonsense, Theodore!" she said, "they can't possibly tell whether I am meeting their gaze or not, or even shutting my eyes—for, of course, I shall be wearing a veil."

But I should not—and it really did not seem fair. "I rather thought of putting on a green shade myself," I said. It had only just occurred to me.

"Don't be absurd, Theodore!" she replied. "What can you want with a green shade?"

"My eyes are not strong," I said, "and with those electric lights so close to the cage, I might blink or even close my eyes. A green shade, like your bridal veil, would conceal the act!"

"As if anybody ever heard of a bridegroom with a green shade over his eyes! I certainly will not enter that cage if I am to be made publicly ridiculous!"

"Do I understand," I said, very gravely, "that you refuse to enter the lion-cage?"

"With a man in a green shade? Most certainly I refuse. Not otherwise."

"Then you will sacrifice my life to mere appearances? Ah, Lurana, that is only one more proof that vanity—not love—has led you to this marriage!"

"Why don't you own at once that you'd give anything to get out of it, Theodore?"

"It is you," I retorted, "you, Lurana, who are secretly dreading the ordeal, and you are trying to throw the responsibility of giving up the whole thing on me—it's not fair, you know!"

"I want to give up the whole thing? Theodore, you know that isn't true!"

"Children, children!" said the Professor, who had been a silent and unnoticed witness of our dispute till then, "What is this talk about giving up the marriage? I implore you to consider the consequences, if the wedding is broken off now by your default. You will be mobbed by a justly indignant crowd, which will probably wreck the hall as a sign of their displeasure. You are just now the two most prominent and popular persons in the United Kingdom—you will become the objects of universal derision. You will ruin that worthy and excellent man, Mr Sawkins, offend Archibald Chuck, and do irretrievable damage to Miss Rakestraw's prospects of success in journalism. Of myself I say nothing, though I may mention that the persons who have paid me fancy prices for the few seats which the management placed at my disposition will infallibly demand restitution and damages. I might even be forced to recover them from you, Theodore. On the other hand, by merely facing a hardly appreciable danger for a very few minutes, you cover yourselves with undying glory, you gain rich and handsome wedding gifts, which I hear the proprietors intend to bestow upon you; you receive an ovation such as is generally reserved for Royal nuptials; and yet you, Theodore, would forfeit all this—for what? For a green shade, which would probably only serve to infuriate the animals?"

This had not struck me before, and I could not help seeing that there was something in it.

"I give up the shade," I said; "but I do think that Lurana is in such a nervous and overstrung condition just now that it is not safe for her to enter the cage without a medical certificate."

Lurana laughed. "What for, Theodore? To satisfy the lions? Don't distress yourself on my account—I am perfectly well. At the appointed time I shall present myself at the—the altar. If you are not there to receive me, to stand by my side in the sight of all, you lose me for ever. A de Castro can never marry a Craven."

She looked so splendid as she said this that I felt there was no peril in the world that I would not face to gain her, that life without her would be unendurable.

Since she was as resolved as ever on this project, I must see it out, that was all, and trust to luck to pull me through. Onion would be there—and he understood lions; and, besides, there was always the bare chance of the ceremony being stopped at the eleventh hour.

I left early, knowing that I should require a good night's rest, and Lurana and I parted, on the understanding that our next meeting would be at the Agricultural Hall on the following afternoon.

Whether it was due to a cup of coffee I had taken at the Professor's, or to some other cause, I do not know, but I had a wretched night, sleeping very literally in fits and starts, and feeling almost thankful when it was time to get up.

A cold bath freshened me up wonderfully, and, as they naturally did not expect me in the City on my wedding-day, I had the whole morning to myself, and decided to get through it by taking a brisk walk. Before starting, I sent a bag containing my wedding garments to the Agricultural Hall, where a dressing room had been reserved for me, and then I started, viâ the Seven Sisters Road, for Finsbury Park.

As I passed an optician's shop, I happened to see, hanging in the window, several pairs of coloured spectacles, one of which I went in and bought, and walked on with a sense of reassurance. Through the medium of such glasses a lion would lose much of his terrors, and would, at the same time, be unable to detect any want of firmness in my gaze; indeed, if a wild beast can actually be dominated by a human eye, how much more should he be so when that eye is reinforced by a pair of smoked spectacles!

My recollection of the rest of that walk is indistinct. I felt no distress, only a kind of stupor. I tried to fix my thoughts on Lurana, on her strange beauty, and the wondrous fact that in a very few hours the ceremony, which was to unite us, would be, at all events, commenced. But at times I had a pathetic sense of the irony which decreed that I, a man of simple tastes and unenterprising disposition, should have fallen hopelessly in love with the only young woman in the United Kingdom capable of insisting on being married in a wild-beast cage.

It seemed hard, and I remember envying quite ordinary persons—butchers, hawkers, errand-boys, crossing-sweepers, and the like, for their good fortune in not being engaged to spend any part of that afternoon in a den of forest-bred African lions.

However, though there was nothing about the intentions of the Home Office in the early editions of the evening papers, the officials might be preparing a dramatic coup for the last moment. I was determined not to count upon it—but the thought of it kept me up until the time when I had to think of returning, for the idea of flight never for an instant presented itself to me. I was on parôle as it were, and I preferred death by Lurana's side to dishonour and security without her.

So anxious was I not to be late, and also to discover whether any communication from the Home Secretary had reached the manager, that I almost hurried back to Islington. I was admitted to the Hall by a private entrance, and shown to the kind of unroofed cabin in which I was to change, and which, being under the balcony and at some distance from the gangway between the stables and the ring, was comparatively private and secluded.

Here, after asking an assistant to let Mr Niono know I had arrived, and would like to see him, I waited. The Circus had begun, as I knew from the facts that the blare of the orchestrions was hushed, and that a brass band overhead began and left off with the abruptness peculiar to Circus music.

Screens of board and canvas hid the auditorium from view, but I was conscious of a vast multitude on the other side, vociferous and in the best of humours.

Between the strains of the orchestra and the rattling volleys of applause, I heard the faint stamping and trampling from the stables, and, a sound that struck a chill to my heart—the prolonged roar of exasperation and ennui which could only proceed from a bored lion.

Then there was a rap at the door, which made me start, and Niono burst in.

"So you've found your way here," he said. "Feeling pretty fit? That's the ticket! The bride ain't arrived yet, so you've lots of time."

"You've heard nothing from the Home Office yet, I suppose?" I asked.

"Not a word—and, between you and me, I made sure they meant to crab the show. You've the devil's own luck!"

"I have, indeed," I said, with feeling. "Still, we mustn't be too sure—they may stop us yet!"

"They may try it on—but our men have got their instructions. If they did come now, they wouldn't get near the ring till it was all over, so don't you worry yourself about that."

I said everything seemed to have been admirably arranged. "By the way," I added, "where have you put the tiger?"

"Do you mean old Rajah?" he said; and I replied that I did mean old Rajah.

"Why, he's all right—in the cage along with the others—where did you suppose he'd be—loose?"

"I particularly requested," I explained, "that he might be put somewhere else during the wedding. Mademoiselle promised that it should be seen to."

"It's nothing to do with Ma'amsell," he said, huffily; "she don't give orders here, Ma'amsell don't."

"I mean, she promised to mention the matter to you," I said, more diplomatically.

"She never said nothing about it to me," he replied; "I expect she forgot."

"I can only say it was extremely careless of her," I said. "The fact is, I have my doubts whether that tiger is to be trusted."

"Well, you never can trust a tiger same as you can a lion," he replied, candidly, "so I won't deceive you. But old Rajah ain't so particular nasty—as tigers go."

"He may not be," I said, "but, in Miss de Castro's interests, I must beg you to shift him into some other cage till this affair is over. I can't allow her to run any unnecessary risk."

"I don't say you're wrong," he answered, "I wish I'd known before, I'd have asked the gov'nor."

"Ask him now," I urged, "surely you can put the tiger back in the hospital cage for an hour or two."

"The Jaguar's in there," he said; "he was a bit off colour, so we put him there this morning. And if them two got together, there'd be the doose's delight!"

"Couldn't you put him somewhere else, then?" I suggested.

"I might ha' shunted him on to the Armadillo at a pinch," he said thoughtfully, "he wouldn't ha' taken any notice, but the gov'nor would have to be consulted first,—and he's engaged in the ring. Besides, it would take too much time to move old Rajah now—you must put up with him, that's all. You'll be right enough if you keep your head and stick close to me. I've taken care they've all had a good dinner. I say," he broke off suddenly, "you're looking uncommon blue."

"I don't feel nervous," I said, "at least, not more nervous than a man ought to feel who's just about to be married. If you mean to suggest that I'm going to show the white feather—!"

"Not you," he said, "what would you get by it, you know? After billing this affair all over the town, we can't afford to disappoint the public, and if I saw you hanging back—why I'm blest if I wouldn't carry you into the cage myself."

I retorted angrily that I would not put him to that inconvenience, that I was as cool as he was, and that I did not understand his remark that I was looking blue.

"Lord, what a touchy chap you are!" he cried; "I meant looking blue about the jaw, that's all. If I was you, I'd have a clean shave. It's enough to put any lady off if she sees you with a chin like the barrel of a musical-box."

Somehow I had omitted to shave myself as usual that morning, intending to get shaved later, but had forgotten to look for a hairdresser's shop during my walk.

"You'll find a razor in that drawer," he said, "if you don't mind making shift with cold water, for there's no one about to fetch you any hot. Now I must be off and get into my own togs. Make yourself at home, you know. I'll give you another call later on."

Perhaps the razor was blunt, perhaps it was the cold water, anyhow I inflicted a gash on the extreme point of my chin which bled profusely. I dabbed and sluiced, but nothing I could do seemed to check the flow; it went on, obstinate and irrepressible. I was still forlornly mopping when Niono returned in his braided jacket, tights and Hessian boots, whistling a tune.

"The bride's just driven up," he announced, "looking like a picture—what pluck she's got! I wish I was in your shoes! Ma'amsell's taken her to her room. My word, though, you've given yourself a nasty cut; got any spider's web about you? Stops it in no time."

As I do not happen to go about festooned in cobwebs, his suggestion was of little practical value, and so I intimated rather sharply.

"Well, don't get in a fluster," he said, "we're only a couple of turns off the Cage Act as it is; you slip into them spicy lavender trousers and that classy frock-coat of yours as quick as you can, and I'll try if I can't borrow a bit of courtplaster off one of our ladies."

I had just put on a clean shirt when he was back again; "I could only get goldbeater's skin," he remarked, "and precious little of that, so be careful with it. And the parson's come, and would like to have a look at the licence."

I handed him the document, and tried to apply the goldbeater's skin, which curled and shrivelled, and would stick to nothing but my fingers—and still the hæmorrhage continued.

"It's all over your shirt now!" said the lion-tamer, as if I was doing it on purpose. "I wouldn't have had this happen for something. Why, I've known 'em get excited with the smell of blood, let alone the sight of it."

"Do you mean the lions?" I inquired, with a faint sick sensation.

"Well, it was the tiger my mind was running on more," was his gloomy reply.

My own mind began to run on the tiger too, and a most unpleasant form of mental exercise it was.

"After all," said Niono with an optimism that sounded a trifle forced, "there's no saying. He mayn't spot it. None of 'em mayn't."

"But what do you think yourself?" I could not help asking.

"I couldn't give an opinion till we get inside," he answered, "but we'll have the red hot irons handy in case he tries on any of his games. And if you can't stop that chin of yours," he added, taking a wrapper from his own neck and tossing it to me, "you'd better hide it in this—they'll only think you've got a sore throat or something. But do hurry up. I'm just going to see the old elephant put in the shafts, and then I'll come back for you, so don't dawdle."

Once more I was alone; I felt so chilly that I put on my old coat and waistcoat again, for I did not venture to touch my new suit until my chin left off bleeding, and it seemed inexhaustible, though the precious minutes were slipping by faster and faster.

The great building had grown suddenly silent; I could almost feel the air vibrating with the suppressed excitement of the vast unseen crowd which was waiting patiently for the lions, and Lurana—and me.

Soon I heard a voice—probably a menagerie assistant's—in the passage outside, and presently a shuffling tread approaching, and then I perceived towering above the wooden partition, a huge grey bulk, ridged and fissured like a mountain side, and touched where the light fell on it with a mouldy bloom—it was the elephant on his way to be attached to the lion-cage!

I stared helplessly up at his uncouth profile, with the knobby forehead worn to a shiny black, and the sardonic little eye that met mine with a humorous intelligence, as though recommending me to haste to the wedding.

He plodded past, and I realised that I had no time to change now; my new wedding suit was a useless extravagance—I must go to the altar as I was. Niono would be back to fetch me in a moment. Lurana would never forgive me for keeping her waiting.

Hastily I wound the muffler round my neck till my chin was hidden in its folds, and put on my hat. Could I have mislaid the spectacles? No, thank heaven, they were in the pocket of my great coat. I put them on, and my wedding toilet—such as it was—was complete.

Then I cast a hurried glance at myself in a tarnished mirror nailed against the matchboarding, and staggered back in dismay. I was not merely unrecognisable; I was—what is a thousand times worse—ridiculous!

Yes, no bridegroom in the world could hope to make a creditable appearance with his nose only just showing above a worsted comforter and his eyes hidden behind a pair of smoked spectacles. It was enough to make any lion roar—the audience would receive me with howls!

I had been prepared—I was still prepared—for Lurana's dear sake, to face the deadliest peril. But to do so with a total loss of dignity; to be irresistibly comic in the supreme crisis, to wrestle with wild beasts to the accompaniment of peals of Homeric laughter—would any lover in the world be capable of heroism such as that?

True, I might remove the spectacles—but in that case I could not trust my nerve; or I might take off the muffler but then I could not trust the tiger. And in either case I should be courting not only my own destruction, but that of one whose life was far dearer to me than my own.

I asked myself solemnly whether I had the right to endanger her safety, simply from a selfish unwillingness to appear grotesque in her eyes and those of the audience. The answer was what every rightminded reader will have foreseen.

And, seeing that the probability was that Lurana would absolutely decline to go through the ceremony at all with the guy I now appeared (for had she not objected even to my assuming a green shade, which was, comparatively, becoming), it was obvious that only one alternative remained, and that I took.

Cautiously opening the door of my cabin, I looked up and down the passage. At one end I could just see the elephant surrounded by a crowd of grooms and helpers, who were presumably harnessing him to the cage and were too far away or too much engaged to notice me. At the other were a few deserted stalls and rifle-galleries, whose proprietors had all gone to swell the crowd of spectators who were waiting to see as much as they could of my wedding, and it began to seem likely that they would see very little indeed.

I was about to make for the nearest exit when I remembered that it would probably be guarded, so, assuming as far as possible the air of an ordinary visitor, I slipped quietly up a broad flight of stairs, on each of which was a recommendation to try somebody's "Pink Pills for Pale People," and gained the upper gallery without attracting attention.

I felt instinctively that my best chance of escaping detection was to mingle with the crowd, and besides, I was naturally curious to know how the affair would end, so, seeing a door and pigeon-hole with the placard "Balcony Seats, Sixpence," I went in, and was lucky enough to secure the only cane bottom chair left in the back row.

After removing my spectacles, I had a fairly good view of the ring below, with its brown tan enclosed by a white border cushioned along the top in faded crimson. The reserved stalls were all full, and beyond the barriers, the crowd swayed and surged in a dense black mass. Nobody was inside the ring except a couple of nondescript grooms in scarlet liveries, who hung about with an air of growing embarrassment. The orchestra opposite was reiterating "The Maiden's Prayer" with a perseverance that at length got upon the nerves of the audience, which began to stamp suggestively.

"It's a swindle," said a husky man, who was obviously inclined to scepticism, and also sherry, "a reg'lar take in! There won't be nobody married in a lion's cage—I've said so all along."

"Oh, it's too soon to say that yet!" I replied soothingly, though I had reasons for being of the same opinion, "they're a little behind time, that's all."

"I dunno what it is they're behind," he said,—"but they don't mean comin' out. There, what did I tell you?"

One of the grooms, obeying instructions from without, had just gone to the Indicator-post, removed the number corresponding with that of the wedding programme, and substituted another, which was the signal for a general uproar.

A carpet was spread for a performance by a "Bender," who made his appearance in a tight suit of green spangles, as the "Marvellous Boy Serpent," and endeavoured to wile away the popular discontent by writhing in and out of the rungs of a chair, and making a glittering pincushion of himself. In vain, for they would have none of him, and the poor youth had to return at last amidst a storm of undeserved hissing.

Another long wait followed, and the indignation grew louder. So infectious is the temper of a mob that I actually caught myself growing impatient, and banging loudly on the floor with my umbrella—just as my neighbours were doing!

All at once, to my extreme bewilderment, the stamping and hooting changed to tumultuous applause, the band began to bray out an air that was apparently intended for "The Voice that Breathed," the barriers were thrown open, and the great elephant lumbered into the arena drawing the cage.

The brute had an enormous wedding favour attached to each side of his tusks, and all the animals in the cage, down to the very tiger, were wearing garlands of artificial orange-blossom, a touch of sentiment which seemed to go straight to the hearts of the people.

But even while I looked down into the cage, with much the same reflection as that of John Bradford of old, that there, but for special grace, I might myself be figuring, I was astounded by the audacity of the management.

Could they really imagine that an intelligent and enlightened audience like this would be pacified by anything less than the spectacle they had paid to witness—a marriage solemnised in a den of lions? And how did they propose to perform a ceremony at which, as they must be fully aware by this time, the bridegroom would be conspicuous by his absence? No, it might be magnificent, but it was not business.

I was still speculating, when a kind of small procession entered the arena. First came Mr Sawkins, with the Reverend Ninian, looking rather like a cheap Cranmer; next was a smart-looking person in a well-cut frock-coat and lavender trousers that I seemed to have seen before. It was my wedding suit; the wearer had gummed on a moustache and short side-whiskers which gave him a spurious resemblance to myself, but if nobody else knew him, I did—it was Onion, the Lion King!

And the next moment, I received a still greater shock, as Professor Polkinghorne followed with the lofty bearing of a Virginius, and on his arm was a slender shrinking figure, which, in spite of the veil she wore, I knew too well could be no other than Lurana.

"There's the bridegroom, d'ye see!" explained my hoarse neighbour; "he's a deal better lookin' than the pictures they've drawed of him in the papers. But he's as pale as plaster, he'll back out of it at the last moment—you just see if he don't!"

But I knew Niono better. I remembered his open admiration of Lurana, his envy at my good fortune, I felt convinced that his pallor was merely due to the absence of rouge and the fear that he would not succeed in his daring imposture. For I saw now that he had been planning to supplant me from the first; hence his attempts to shake my nerve, and, when they failed, hence his treacherous loan of a blunt razor. He was staking everything on the chance that the bride's natural agitation, and the thickness of her veil would prevent her from suspecting that he was a fraudulent bridegroom until the ceremony was over, while the audience, not expecting to see a Lion King in a tall hat, would be equally deceived.

"Pore young things!" said a stout female in front, with a nodding feather in her bonnet; "it's to be 'oped there won't be any unpleasantness, I'm sure. I'm 'alf sorry I came."

There was time even yet; I had but to rise, denounce the usurper, and take my rightful place at Lurana's side. I felt strongly impelled to do so; I actually stood up and tried to speak. But I realised that it was hopeless to attempt to make my feeble voice heard above the thunders of applause, even if excitement and emotion had not rendered me speechless. Besides, what satisfactory explanation of my present position could I offer? I sat down again with a sense of spellbound helplessness.

I looked on as the great arc-lamps were lowered, hissing and buzzing, to the level of the cage, and the Reverend Mr Skipworth prepared to ascend the inverted white tub that was to serve him as a reading-desk, and the unscrupulous Onion took the bride by the hand and conducted her to the steps which led to the door of the lion-cage.

"They're never goin' in among all them lions without nobody with them!" cried the stout lady. "It's downright temptin' of Providence, that it is!"

"Don't you be afraid," said the cynical man. "They ain't goin' in. Just look at that now!"

As he spoke two persons in plain clothes, who had apparently been waiting for this moment, stepped over the barrier from the shilling stalls into the ring, and, from their gestures, seemed to be insisting that the wedding should not take place inside the cage at all events.

There was an animated dispute in the ring; Niono blustered, Lurana pleaded, Sawkins expostulated, and the professor and Archibald Chuck (who had contrived to push himself into the party) argued, while Miss Rakestraw filled page after page of her reporter's note-book, and the Rev. Ninian sat upon his tub with meekly folded hands, looking more than ever like a martyr who knew himself to be incombustible.

The audience booed, and hissed, and yelled with natural rage and disappointment; the lions remained unmoved, blinking behind their bars, with crossed forepaws, and an air of serene indifference.

"I told yer there wasn't going to be no blooming wedding!" said my husky friend. "It's a reg'lar put-up job, that's what it is!"

It was possible; but whether the interrupters of the proceedings were hired supers or genuine officials, it was equally clear that there would be no wedding inside the cage.

How bitterly I regretted that by yielding to an irresistible impulse I had forfeited the right to stand by Lurana's side at this supreme moment! I could have done so with absolute impunity; I should have won a lifelong reputation for courage; Lurana herself would have owned that I had done all that was possible to gratify her whim, and would have consented to marry me in the orthodox fashion.

Whereas, here I was, separated from her by impassable barriers, in the ignominious seclusion of a back seat! However, this official prohibition had at least solved one of my difficulties; it had rendered it unnecessary for me to interfere personally.

The storm of indignation rose to a hurricane when the entire wedding party filed out of the arena with the officials, doubtless to discuss the matter in greater privacy.

The stout lady with the feather was particularly annoyed. "Why shouldn't the two young parties be allowed to please themselves?" she wanted to know. "It was their wedding, not the Government's. But it was always the way whenever she came out for a little amusement. Somethink was bound to go wrong."

Another long interval, during which the wildest disorder reigned unchecked, the crowd, with the irrationality of an angry mob, actually throwing pieces of orange-peel at the unoffending lions as the only creatures within the range of their displeasure. The hubbub was at its height when Sawkins reappeared and held up his hand for some time in vain before he could obtain a hearing. Then he addressed the audience as follows:

"Ladies and Gentlemen," he said, "certain individuals claiming to represent the Home Office and the London County Council" (here there were groans, and my neighbour remarked disgustedly, that "that was what came of returning those Progressives") "have protested against a wedding in the cage as involving danger to the principal parties concerned." (Loud cries of "Shame!" and general uproar.) "I have the honour and pleasure to announce that we have succeeded in convincing these gentlemen that the proposed ceremony is no more open to objection than the ordinary performance, and that they have no legal power to prohibit it. Consequently the marriage will now be celebrated in the cage of forest-bred African lions, as advertised."

The revulsion of feeling after this most unexpected announcement was instant and tremendous; all hearts seemed touched with generous compunction for their uncharitable suspicions, and the hall rang with tumultuous cheers.

For myself, I could not share the general exhilaration. This preposterous wedding was permitted after all, and, unless Lurana's heart failed her at the critical instant, she would inevitably be lost to me for ever! I might still interpose; indeed I should have done so at all costs, but for a timely remembrance that no action I took now would regain her.

She might have been in ignorance before—but in the course of this delay she must have learnt that I had failed her, she must have accepted the lion-tamer as a substitute, and, even if I were to present myself, she would only inform me that my place was already filled. I had too much spirit to risk a public snub of that kind, so I stayed where I was. It cannot have fallen to many men's lot to look on as passive spectators at their own wedding—but what choice had I?

There was a deathlike silence as Niono slipt the bolt and gallantly handed the bride into the cage. She stepped in as collectedly as if it had been an ordinary Registry Office, and the great tawny beasts retreated sullenly to the other end, where they stood huddled in a row, while the Rev. Ninian, mounting his tub, read an abbreviated form of service in a voice which was quite inaudible in the balcony.

I tried to turn my eyes away from the scene that was taking place in that grim cage, and the two figures that were so calmly confronting those formidable brutes—but I felt compelled to look. And it was mortifying to see how trifling after all was the danger they incurred. I am afraid I almost wished that one of the animals would give some trouble—I don't mean of course by any actual attack—but by just enough display of ferocity to make Lurana understand what they might do.

But they never even attempted to cross the pole which had been thrust across the cage as a barrier. I was never told there would be a pole! They looked on, mystified—as well they might be—by proceedings to which they were totally unaccustomed, but still impressed, and sleepily solemn. Even the tiger behaved with irreproachable decorum.

I understood then what Onion had been careful not to mention; their food had been doctored in some way. If I had only known! Anybody could beard a hocussed lion!

And soon the words which made that couple man and wife were pronounced, or rather mumbled—for the Rev. Ninian would have been none the worse for a course of lessons from old Polkinghorne—and the newly-wedded pair came out of the cage without so much as a scratch, to the triumphant blare of the "Wedding March." There was frantic applause as the Professor embraced the bride with an emotion that struck me as overdone, while the Rev. Ninian, Miss Rakestraw, and Chuck, offered their congratulations and Mr Sawkins presented the happy couple with a silver biscuit-box (it may have been electro-plated), and a Tantalus spirit case.

But for that unfortunate slip of the razor, those gifts would have been mine—but I was in no mood to think of that just then, when I had lost what was so infinitely more precious.

I looked on dully till the party left the arena, declining with excellent taste to return in answer to repeated calls and bow their acknowledgments, and then, as the electric lights were hoisted up again and the elephant was led in to remove the lion's cage, I thought it was time to go.

It was all over; there was nothing to stay for now, and most of the people were leaving, so I joined the crowd which streamed down the staircase and along the broad passage to the main exit. Once in the open air, I hurried blindly past the flaring shops in the High Street, neither knowing nor caring where I was going, with only one thought possessing my numbed brain—how different it might all have been if only things had happened otherwise!

Wherever I looked I saw Lurana's lovely scornful face and flashing eyes painted with torturing vividness on the murky air. How flat and stale all existence would be for me henceforth! Life with Lurana might not have been all sunshine; it might have had its storms, even its tempests—but at least it would never have been dull!

I cursed the treachery which had induced her to link herself for life with a lion-tamer. Happy, I knew she could not be, for of one thing I was confident—she loved me; not perhaps with the passionate single-hearted devotion I felt for her, but still with a love she would never feel for any other. Perhaps she was already beginning to repent her desertion of me, and wishing she could undo that rash irrevocable act.

I was pounding up Highgate Hill, with no object beyond escaping by active motion the demons of recollection and regret that haunted me—when suddenly, as I gained the top of the hill, a thought struck me. Was the act irrevocable after all? Was it so absolutely certain that this Onion had the legal right to claim her as his wife?

He had certainly personated me. Had he borrowed, not only my frock coat, and trousers, but also my name for the ceremony? If he had, and if Lurana was, as she could hardly help being, aware of the fact, it did not require much acquaintance with the law to know that there was a chance, at all events, of getting the Court to declare the marriage null and void.

But he might have been married in his own name; I could not tell, owing to the indistinctness of Mr Skipworth's utterance, only Lurana or those in their immediate neighbourhood could say. I must know that first; I must examine the register, if there was one, and then, if—if Lurana wished to be saved, I might be able to save her.

I knew that a sort of wedding high-tea had been prepared at Canonbury Square, where the whole party would be assembled by this time, and I hurried back to Canonbury Square as fast as the tramcar would take me. My blood was roused; she would not be Niono's if I could prevent it. I would snatch her from him, even if I had to do so across the wedding-cake!

But when I reached the well-known door and raised the familiar knocker—a fist clutching a cast-iron wreath—in my trembling fingers, there were no sounds of festivity within; the house was dark and deserted.

I waited in the bitter January air; the street lamp opposite—the identical one under which Lurana had first agreed to marry me—flickered at every gust of the night wind, as though troubled on my account. They must have transferred the feast to the Circus, or to some adjacent restaurant; evidently there was no one there.

I was just turning hopelessly away, when I heard the bolt being withdrawn, and the door was opened by a maid.

"Where is your mistress?" I asked breathlessly. I could not bring myself to ask for Lurana as Mrs Onion.

"In the drawing-room, upstairs," was the unexpected reply, "with the 'istericks."

So long as she was not with Niono, I cared little; I bounded up, and found her alone.

As I entered, she raised her flushed, tear-stained face from the shabby sofa on which she had thrown herself. "Go away!" she cried, "why do you come near me now? You have no right—do you hear?—no right!"

"I know," I said humbly enough, "I deserve this, no doubt; and yet, if you knew all, you would find excuses for me, Lurana!"

"None, Theodore," she said; "if you had really loved me, you would never have deserted me!"

"I could not help myself," I retorted; "and really, Lurana, if it comes to desertion—!"

"Ah, what is the use of wrangling about whose fault it was," she moaned, "now, when we have both wrecked our lives! At least, I know I've wrecked mine! Why was I so insane as to set my heart on our being married in a den of disgusting lions? If you had only been firmer, Theodore, instead of giving way as you did!"

"At least it was not cowardice," I said. "When I show you the state of my chin——"

"Theodore!" she cried, with a little scream, "you are hurt! Tell me; was it the tiger?"

"It was not the tiger," I said. "Never mind that now. I was betrayed by that infernal Onion, Lurana. I never knew till it was too late—you do believe me, don't you?"

"I do; we were both deceived, Theodore. I should never have acted as I did if that horrid Frenchwoman hadn't told me—Oh, what would I not give if all this had never been?"

"If you are truly sincere," I began, "in wishing this unlucky marriage cancelled—"

"If I am! Are you, Theodore? Oh, if only there is a way!"

"There may be, Lurana. It all depends on whether my name was used at the ceremony or not. Try to recollect and tell me."

"But I can't, Theodore. You were there—you must know!"

"Mr Skipworth wouldn't speak up; and I was much farther away than you were."

"Than I was, Theodore! But—but I wasn't there at all!"

"Not present at your own wedding?" I cried, "but I saw you!"

"It was not me!" she said, "it was Mlle. Léonie. Is it possible you didn't know?"

My heart leaped. "For heaven's sake, explain, Lurana; let us have no more concealments."

"When I arrived," she said, "Mademoiselle explained about the tiger, and how sorry she was it was too late to remove it, since she understood I had an antipathy to tigers; and I said, not at all, I adored tigers, so she took me to see the cage, and I—I only tried to tickle the tiger, but he was so dreadfully cross about it—I nearly fainted. And she said it was simply madness for me to go in, and that you were every bit as frightened as I was."

"She had no right to say that," I said; "it's absolutely untrue!"

"I know, Theodore," she replied; "you have proved that you, at least, are no coward—but I believed her then. And I wrote you a line to say that I had altered my mind, and did not think it right to expose you or myself to such danger, and that I would wait for you by the Myddelton Statue. She promised to give you the letter at once!"

"I never got it," I said.

"No, she took care you should not. And I waited for you—how long I don't know—hours, it seemed—but you never came! Then I saw the people beginning to come out, and—and I went across and asked someone whether there had been any marriage or not, and he said, 'Yes, it had gone off without any accident, the bridegroom looked pale but was plucky enough, and so was the bride, though he couldn't tell how she looked, because of her veil.' And then of course, I knew that the deceitful cat had taken my place and managed to make you marry her! And at first I wanted to go back and stab her with my hat pin, but I hadn't one sharp enough, so I came home instead. And oh, Theodore, I do feel so ashamed! After boasting so much of my Spanish blood, and taunting you with being afraid as I did, to think that you should have shown the truer courage after all!"

I could not triumph over her then; I was too happy. "Courage, my darling, is a merely relative quality," I said. "Heaven forbid that we should be held accountable for the state of our nerves—even the bravest of us."

"But this marriage, Theodore," she said, "what can you do to have it set aside?"

"Do! Nothing," I replied; "after what you have told me, I no longer care to try."

"You despise me, then, because I broke down at the critical moment?"

"Not at all. I can never be grateful enough to you!"

"Grateful! Then do you mean to say you prefer that coarse, middle-aged, lion-taming person to me, Theodore?"

"Lurana," I said, "prepare yourself for a great surprise—a pleasant surprise. If anybody is now that lady's lawful husband it is Niono—not I; and a very suitable match too," I added (I saw now why the authorities had been compelled to waive their objections to it). "The fact is, I never went into the cage at all."

"You didn't go into the cage, Theodore! but how, why?"

"Do you imagine," I asked, "can you really suppose I should be capable of entering that cage with anybody but yourself, Lurana? How little you know me! Of course I declined!"

"But you didn't know I had run away then, Theodore! Why, you thought only a few minutes ago I was the person Mr Niono married! Perhaps you will kindly explain?"

For the moment I was in a fix, but I saw that the moment had arrived for perfect candour, and accordingly I told her the facts pretty much as they have been set down here.

She could hardly blame me for having behaved precisely as she herself had done, or refuse to admit that by taking any other course I should have imperilled our joint happiness, and yet I thought I could see that, with feminine unreason, she was just a little disappointed with me.

The true explanation of that marriage, if it was a marriage, in the den of lions, I have never been able to discover, nor for that matter have I been particularly curious to inquire whether Onion attempted to get rid of me in order to secure Lurana; whether Mdlle. Léonie played upon Lurana's fears with the hope of becoming my bride, or his; or whether the Lion King and his fellow artist gallantly sacrificed themselves to get the management out of a difficulty, I don't know, and, as I say, I haven't cared to ask.

But however it was, they were ably seconded by old Polkinghorne, who was naturally unwilling to be called upon to refund the money he had got for his free tickets, and by Miss Rakestraw and Archibald Chuck, whose reputations were also more or less concerned.

Nevertheless, although every effort was made to keep the public off the scent, and the circus people behaved, I am bound to say, with commendable discretion, sundry garbled versions of the facts did get about, and altogether Lurana and I have found the task of denying or correcting them such a constant nuisance that I have felt compelled, as I said at starting, to furnish, once for all, a statement of what actually occurred.

Now that it is written I have no more to add, except to append a cutting from an announcement which appeared not long ago in the principal papers. The arrangements for its publication were entrusted to Archibald Chuck, who I think must have added the last two words on his own responsibility.

Blenkinsop—De Castro.—On the 15th inst., at the Parish Church of St Mary, Islington, by the Rev. Merton Sandford, D.D., Vicar, THEODORE PIDGLEY BLENKINSOP, of Highbury, to LURANA CARMEN DE CASTRO, only daughter of the late Manuel Guzman de Castro, formerly Deputy Sub-Assistant Inspector of Spanish Liquorice to the Government Manufactory at Madrid. No lions.

F. Anstey – A Concise Bibliography

Vice Versa (1882)
The Black Poodle And Other Tales (1884)
The Giant's Robe (1884)
The Tinted Venus (1885)
A Fallen Idol (1886)
Burglar Bill And Other Pieces (1888)
The Pariah (1889)
Voces Populi (1890)
Tourmalin's Time Cheques (1891)
Mr. Punch's Model Music-Hall Songs And Dramas (1892)
The Talking Horse And Other Tales (1892)
The Travelling Companions (1892)
The Man From Blankley's And Other Sketches (1893)
Mr. Punch's Pocket Ibsen (1893)
Under the Rose (1894)
Lyre and Lancet (1895)
The Statement of Stella Maberly, Written By Herself (1896)
Baboo Jabberjee, B. A. (1897)
Puppets At Large (1897)
Love Among The Lions (1898)
Paleface And Redskin (1898)
The Brass Bottle (1900)
A Bayard From Bengal (1902)

Only Toys! (1903)
Salted Almonds (1906)
Winnie, An Everyday Story (1909)
In Brief Authority (1915)
Percy and Others (1915)
The Last Load (1925)
The Would-Be Gentleman (Adapted From Molière's Le Bourgeois gentilhomme) (1927)
The Imaginary Invalid (Adapted From Molière's Le Malade imaginaire) (1929)
Humour and Fantasy (1931)
A Long Retrospect (1936)